When I first read the famous Bluebeard fairytale to Anna, she was very cross. 'If Bluebeard didn't want his bride to look into that room, he shouldn't have given her the key,' she cried. 'Everyone knows that when you are told not to do a particular thing, that is the very thing you just have to do!'

Many years have passed since we first read that story, but Anna's feelings of outrage are still strong.

So why not give him to our brave Tashi, we thought, and see what happens...?

BARBARA FIENBERG

Anna and Barbara Fienberg write the Tashi stories together, making up all kinds of daredevil adventures and tricky characters for him to face. Lucky he's such a clever Tashi.

Kim Gamble is one of Australia's favourite illustrators for children. Together Kim and Anna have made such wonderful books as *The Magnificent Nose and Other Marvels*, *The Hottest Boy Who Ever Lived*, the *Tashi* series, the *Minton* picture books, *Joseph,* and a full colour picture book about their favourite adventurer, *There once was a boy called Tashi.*

First published in 2005
This edition first published in 2006

Allen & Unwin
83 Alexander St
Crows Nest NSW 2065
Australia
Phone: (61 2) 8425 0100
Fax: (61 2) 9906 2218
Email: info@allenandunwin.com
Web: www.allenandunwin.com

National Library of Australia
Cataloguing-in-Publication entry:

Fienberg, Anna.
   Tashi and the forbidden room.

   New cover ed.
   For primary school children.
   ISBN 978 1 74114 964 7.

1. Children's stories, Australian. 2. Tashi (Fictitious character) – Juvenile
fiction. I. Fienberg, Barbara. II. Gamble, Kim. III. Title. (Series: Tashi; 12).

A823.3

Cover and series design by Sandra Nobes
Typeset in Sabon by Tou-Can Design
Printed in Australia by McPhersons Printing Group

10 9 8 7 6 5 4 3 2

Tashi

and the
FORBIDDEN
ROOM

written by
Anna Fienberg
and
Barbara Fienberg

illustrated by
Kim Gamble

ALLEN&UNWIN

Jack hung up his bag in the hatroom and raced into class. 'Sorry I'm late but –'

'You were kidnapped by bandits,' said Mrs Hall.

'Strangled by mummies!' called out Angus Figment.

'Held up by Uncle Joe,' sighed Jack.

Mrs Hall's eyes lit up. 'Uncle Joe? The brave traveller with many tales to tell of secret jungles and famous fishing spots around the world?'

'Yes,' said Jack. 'He's just come back from the Limpopo River in Africa.'

'Ooh!' Mrs Hall bounced on her seat with excitement. 'I've only ever *read* about Africa. How I would like to *go* there! Well, class, today we will have a chance to be explorers ourselves. We're going to choose a pen friend – someone who lives far away. You will write telling them about your life and they'll write back about theirs. Now let's look at this marvellous world of ours and think where we would most like to explore.'

Jack put up his hand. 'Can we choose our own person to write to?'

'Well, yes. And would this be someone your Uncle Joe has met?'

'No.'

Mrs Hall waited. She waggled her eyebrows wildly at Jack. But Jack said nothing more.

At morning tea, Jack sat down next to
Tashi. 'I'd like to write to someone from
your village. I bet your grandfather has
seen a lot in his time.'

'Yes, but his English is tricky.'

'I just want to ask him one question:
which one of your adventures he thinks is
the scariest.'

'Hmm,' said Tashi, unwrapping his rice
cake.

'Do you think it would be the same
one you'd pick?'

'No. The one I'd pick stays in a small dark corner of my mind. I try not to think of it, but a certain monster of a man will always haunt me.'

Jack was silent for a moment. 'Is this the man you started to tell me about in the lift? Bluebeard?'

Tashi nodded. 'He was so full of venom, he could kill a snake.'

'Gosh,' said Jack. 'What was so bad about him?'

'Well, it all began with the castle on the hill,' said Tashi. He took a deep breath. 'The castle had stood empty for many years. It had twenty-three bedrooms, upstairs and downstairs, and they were dark and dusty with cobwebs. But one day Second Aunt called to tell us that she had just met the new owner. He was a wealthy merchant, she said, tall and

handsome, with hair as blue-black as a
raven's wing.'

'Bluebeard!'

Tashi shuddered. 'The colour of his
beard gave him his name. After this story
is told, Jack, let's not talk about him
again. I am only telling you because you
are my best friend.'

Jack nodded gravely.

'Well, at first we were excited about the new owner of the castle – you know, a mysterious stranger from outside the village – and we couldn't wait to see him for ourselves. We were even more excited when Lotus Blossom burst in with news.

'"Guess what!" she yelled. "You'll never guess, no you won't in a million moons – "

'Grandma told her it was rude to interrupt people's dinner, and that if she didn't watch out she'd give her a dose of witch's warts to improve her manners. But then I saw that look in Grandma's eye.

'"Well, now that you're here," she said, "you'd better tell us."

'"It's about the handsome stranger," crowed Lotus Blossom. "I know something *you* don't know!" and she danced around the table.

'Oh, Jack, that girl might be my cousin but sometimes she's more annoying than a wasp in summer!'

'I know what you mean,' nodded Jack. 'I wish I'd had a dose of witch's warts for Uncle Joe this morning.'

'Well, finally Lotus Blossom told us the news. The wealthy new owner had asked her Elder Sister Ho Hum to marry him!

Their father was very pleased, because although Ho Hum was pretty she was such a languid sleepy sort of girl he'd been worried she would never do anything with her life but sit in her comfortable chair and doze.

'Everyone was busy in the next few weeks, helping to clean up and decorate the castle. We had big parties to welcome the stranger. All the villagers said how well Ho Hum had done to find such a husband – everyone except me, that is. On the day I met Bluebeard I saw something that showed me a glimpse of his evil heart.'

'What?'

'Well, it was like this. At one of the parties I noticed Granny White Eyes asking for a cup of water.'

'Oh, I remember her,' said Jack. 'She's the old blind lady who helped you beat the demons.'

'Yes, and I saw Bluebeard fill a cup from the dog's water bowl to give to her! He had a nasty smile. I dashed over and, pretending to be clumsy, knocked it out of her hand. I gave her fresh water, but my heart was heavy.

'It was even heavier the next day when I visited Not Yet at his shop. He was trembling. "Oh, Tashi," he moaned, "that monster Bluebeard was here this morning to collect the shoes he'd left for me to mend. Just because I said they weren't quite ready, he threatened to – " Not Yet's face crumpled. "Tashi, if anything happens to me, I want you to have my hammer with the ebony handle." Not Yet wouldn't say any more. He just bundled me out and locked his door and windows.

'I hurried off to tell Ho Hum what had happened. But she didn't believe me.

'"You've got it wrong, Tashi," she said. "Anyway, everyone gets angry with Not Yet when their shoes aren't ready."

'The next day Ho Hum and Lotus Blossom came to take me on a trip up to the castle. Bluebeard was away on some business in the city and he'd given the castle keys to his bride so she could make sure that the new bed had arrived.

'While Ho Hum had a little rest, Lotus Blossom and I explored the gardens, ran up and down the stairs and shouted along the corridors. We came back for Ho Hum, and looked into each of the twenty-three rooms until we arrived at the tower at the top of the castle. The door was locked.

'"We can't go into that room," said Ho Hum. "Not ever."

'"Why not?" asked Lotus Blossom. "What can be in there? Don't you want to know?" She knelt down to look through the keyhole. "I can't see anything; it's blocked. Oh please, Ho Hum, let's have one little peek inside."

'I think Ho Hum had been just waiting for someone to persuade her. She had the right key ready in her hand! When she opened the door, we all gasped. There were hundreds of wooden chests stacked with treasure, cloths of gold and peacock fans.

'"Look," cried Lotus Blossom, "over there! That's the cabinet of jade figures that was stolen from the Baron last week. Ho Hum, it seems that you are marrying a robber!"

'At that very moment I heard faint cries coming from behind some carved screens. Lotus Blossom and I pushed them aside and stood frozen with horror.

'Five young women were hanging by their wrists, tied to iron rings set in the wall behind them!

'My heart started racing and a chill like iced water spread down my back. Not Yet was right – only a monster would do

such a thing. Quickly we went to the girls
and gently tried to undo their straps.
Their faces and arms were white as
ghosts, and when the cruel leather straps
came off the girls cried in agony.

'They knelt on the floor and slowly
told us their stories. One by one they had
married Bluebeard, only to find they
displeased him in some way.

'"My mistake was to sing while I
cleaned the house," sobbed the first girl.
"Bluebeard said singing was for birds,
and birds should be in cages."

"'I served his tea too hot," said the second girl. "My father always liked the way I made tea, but Bluebeard said it burnt his mouth."

"'I talked to a neighbour – " sighed the third girl.

"'I dropped a plate – " whispered the fourth.

'"And I fed a stray cat," said the fifth wife. "Bluebeard punished us all by locking us up. Then one night, when all the village was sleeping, he brought us to this castle. I don't know how many days we have been here, but I am sure he means us to starve to death!"

'"Let's get out of here," Ho Hum said urgently. But we heard a creak on the stairs. Bluebeard's deep, harsh voice floated up to us. Quickly, Ho Hum ducked down behind the cabinet.

'"We'll come back for you," I whispered to the girls, pulling the screen back in place. Lotus Blossom grabbed my hand and we slipped in behind the curtains just as Bluebeard strode into the room.

'He was followed by two men with faces sharp as knives. "Take these boxes down to the cart – oh, that cabinet too –" he snapped. The men lifted the Baron's cabinet and Ho Hum was left staring into the furious eyes of her husband-to-be.

'His face grew dark as a storm. "I knew it!" he hissed. "You have disobeyed me in the one thing I asked of you, just like all the others. Take her away," he growled to one of the men behind him.

'Of course, wouldn't you know it, Lotus Blossom couldn't keep still on hearing that. She sprang out from behind the curtain, yelling at Bluebeard. "What do you mean, *take her away*?" she bellowed. "What are you going to do with Ho Hum? You can't lock her up forever for disobeying you!"

Bluebeard looked at Lotus Blossom
as if she was just a bug on his shoe.
He took his time, considering whether to
squash her or not. "Take them both below
to the room with the barred windows,"
he finally told the men, "then finish
loading the cart." And he marched off,
out the door.

'I waited as the men took the sisters
and the boxes, and when they were gone
I tiptoed out from behind the curtain.
There was only one thing to do and
luckily I had come prepared.

'*Wah*, you should have seen Ho Hum jump as I stepped through the wall.

'"Where did you come from, Tashi?" she gasped.

'"I never did trust that Bluebeard, so I brought my magic shoes and these ghost cakes, in case," I told her.

'We explained to Ho Hum how easy it is to walk through walls once you've eaten a piece of ghost cake. But then we had to decide: which wall to go through now?

'"It's no use going through the door," I whispered, "there's sure to be a guard in the hallway." I listened carefully at the wall of the next room. "We don't want to walk into a roomful of Bluebeard's robbers." I took a deep breath. "I'll go first."

'"No, we'll go together," said Lotus Blossom. So they swallowed their ghost cakes and we all stepped through the wall. INTO A ROOMFUL OF ROBBERS!

'They were sitting around a table with their feet up and for a moment they were stuck to their seats in surprise. I seized a sword from the nearest robber, and I ran up the wall in my magic shoes. I skimmed across the ceiling, swishing the sword round and round my head. I moved so quickly I was just a blur of red coat and whistling sword, bouncing off the walls and floor and ceiling like a demon,

shouting, "Out, out, OUT! Before you
lose your EARS!" The stupefied robbers
fought each other to be first out the door,
and out of the castle.

"'Well done, Tashi," said Ho Hum.
For once she looked quite lively. "That
was...very interesting."

"'We still have to get out of the castle,"
I panted, trying to get my breath. "And
Blubeard won't be so easy to frighten."

'We crept down the hall towards the stairs and we could see the open front door – so inviting! My foot was on the first step when I saw Bluebeard stride into the entry hall from the cellar. He was carrying two more iron rings. Quickly we shrank against the wall and crept back into the shadows.

'A tall vase stood outside the room with the barred windows. I silently pointed to Lotus Blossom and Ho Hum to hide behind it and I squeezed in behind a suit of armour on the other side of the door.

'Bluebeard's face was set and his mouth was grim as he unlocked the door of the room. He stepped inside. We heard a sound of surprise as he looked around and found the sisters missing. Quick as a thunderclap I slammed the door shut. Ho Hum turned the key in the lock just as Bluebeard hurled himself against the door. Too late.

'We raced like the wind down to the village square and straight over to the Warning Bell. People came streaming out of their houses and shops, wanting to know what had happened. As soon as we told them about Bluebeard, they grabbed their shovels and pitchforks and carving knives and we all hurried back to the castle. The cart loaded with treasure was still outside where the robbers had left it. Lotus Blossom ran ahead, climbing the tower to free the poor wives, while I led the way to the room where Bluebeard was held.

'He put up a tremendous fight when
we burst in on him. I'll never forget the
look on his face. He bared his teeth like
a wild dog, and he leapt on the nearest
man, cursing and hurling punches. "Get
out of my way, you miserable wretches,"
he snarled. "My men will be here any
moment to tear you apart!"

'He thrashed his way through the
villagers like an army until four men
linked arms and surrounded him. It took
another four to overpower him and three
more to tie him up in his own chains.

'As he was led away, Lotus Blossom
took Ho Hum's hand. "It's a terrible
thing, Ho Hum. Are you very upset?"

'Ho Hum shivered, looking over at me.
"Just as well you came with us today,
Tashi. I wouldn't have wanted to be wife
number six." She smiled sleepily at Lotus
Blossom. "It wouldn't have been...very
restful."'

Jack snorted. 'That was one mean man,' he said. 'But then, the ghosts you met were monsters too. And that white tiger – he'd have swallowed you whole.'

Tashi stood up and threw his rubbish in the bin.

'If you could choose,' went on Jack, 'would you rather be tied to a tree and eaten slowly by soldier ants or attacked by a lion?'

'Lion,' said Tashi.

'Would you rather die of cold or hot?'

'Cold,' said Tashi after a moment.
'Because you just fall asleep. Fifth Cousin
almost went that way. They found him all
curled up in the snow with a smile on his
face. When they thawed him out he said it
was just like dreaming.'

As they wandered back to the
classroom, Jack and Tashi discussed what
they would do if they ever met anybody
as monsterish as Bluebeard again.

'We could make a book of handy
hints,' said Jack. 'Call it *A Survival Guide
to Monsters*.'

'Would there be a man as evil as
Bluebeard in it?' said Tashi.

'You bet!' said Jack. 'But we
just won't mention his name.'

THE THREE TASKS

'Hi Jack,' called Mum from the laundry, 'how was your day?'

'Good,' Jack called back, flicking off his shoes and opening the fridge.

'Did you show Tashi the letter you got from his grandfather?'

'Yesh,' said Jack.

'Jack? Are you eating that pie for tonight's dinner?' Mum marched into the kitchen and dumped the washing on the table.

'You know the three tasks that Grandfather wrote about in his letter?' began Jack.

'Yes,' nodded Mum. 'He said to ask Tashi about them. So did you hear the whole story? And why did Grandfather ask if you had a dog?'

'Well, Tashi said that after his family, Grandfather's favourite creature in all the world was this dog called Pongo. And Grandfather's favourite Tashi adventure was about Pongo.'

'What, did the dog have to perform the three tasks?' said Mum.

'No,' sighed Jack. 'Do you want to hear the story? I've written most of it down in my *Survival Guide*.'

'So tell me,' said Mum, as she sorted the socks into pairs.

'Well, it was like this,' said Jack. 'One day Tashi was poking about behind Granny White Eyes' house, weeding her garden, when he came across a clump of mandrake plants. Wise-as-an-Owl will be pleased, he thought, and he set out to tell him.'

'What's so good about mandrake plants?' asked Mum.

'Be patient and you'll hear,' said Jack. 'As I was saying, Tashi set off and as he was going through the square he met Lotus Blossom and Ah Chu. "We'll come with you!" they both said, and Tashi agreed. It was a good excuse, of course, to peek inside the wise man's house and have a look at all those strange plants and bubbling beakers.

'But when they arrived it was his son Much-to-Learn who opened the door.

'"You didn't try to pick them I hope?"
Much-to-Learn asked anxiously as Tashi
told him about the mandrake plants.

'"Of course I didn't," said Tashi. "I
knew it would be much too dangerous for
anyone but Wise-as-an-Owl to pull them
up, although I expect you will be able to
do it soon, Much-to-Learn," he added
politely.

'Wise-as-an-Owl came in then and offered them all tea. Tashi said it had an odd taste – spicy, with a kick to it that tingled at the back of your throat after you swallowed. But it was nice and left you feeling calm. Anyway, just as they were leaving, Wise-as-an-Owl drew Tashi aside. He thanked him for coming, and he gave Tashi a little present wrapped in brown paper. Tashi tucked it in his hair, where he often carried precious things.

'As they left, the children could hear Much-to-Learn listing all the magical and important parts of wild mandrake root.

'It was a fine day, so they dawdled along, enjoying the sunshine. The way home took them past the Baron's house and they could smell the delicious scent of flowers on the breeze. The Baron had a beautiful garden – it was a pity no one was allowed to walk in it.

'Tashi said, "Why don't we stop for a
moment. The Baron isn't here and we
could see that new peacock he has been
bragging about."

'"Yes," agreed Lotus Blossom. "I heard
him in the village yesterday. He says it's
the most magnificent bird in the world,
and he's bought a peahen as well. He was
boasting that soon he'd be making
another fortune breeding the most
splendid birds in the country."

'They wandered around the garden, sniffing the orange and lemon blossoms, but there was no sign of the peacock. A joyful bark made them jump and they swung around to see Pongo bounding towards them. Tashi was just bending to throw a stick for him when the Baron came walking up the path.

'"Where is my peacock?" the Baron shouted.

'Pongo barked and as all eyes turned
to him they saw that his jowls and teeth
were covered in blood. Nearby, lying on
the lawn, were two crumpled feathers.

'The Baron roared again with rage and
whipped the dog savagely. Then he
dragged the whimpering Pongo to the
cellar and shut him in. Tashi couldn't help
following a few paces behind and he heard
the Baron shouting, "You've made a meal
of my peacock, Pongo, now let's see how
many meals you miss before you *die*!"
And he slammed the big iron door with
such force that Tashi's ears were ringing.

'Well, you can imagine how Tashi felt going home that night. He couldn't stop thinking about poor Pongo. Tashi's mother wanted to know why he wasn't eating his dinner but when he told her about Pongo, she said no, they couldn't bring him home.

'"Pongo is the Baron's dog, Tashi," she said. "If you take him it would be stealing."

'The next morning Tashi and his friends sneaked down into the cellar to bathe Pongo's cuts and give him some food and water. Tashi had found some left-over chicken necks and egg noodles.

'Ah Chu was sighing – he found it very difficult to watch anyone else eating when he was not. Even a dog. Even if it was a bowl of cold scraps. "Goodness, listen to that," he said thankfully as they heard the clock strike twelve. "It's lunchtime already."

'Tashi grinned. "That's all right. You two go. I'll just stay a few minutes more to give Pongo a bit of friendly company."

'After checking to see if the coast was clear, Ah Chu and Lotus Blossom slipped away home.

'Tashi scratched behind the dog's ears and patted his soft tummy. Pongo made low moaning sounds in his throat and licked Tashi's knees.

'Only a moment later, the door banged open. The Baron glared down at Tashi. "Interfering again, I see, Tashi. Don't you know that once a dog has tasted a live bird you can never trust him again?"

'"Oh Baron, what can I say to make you change your mind?"

'A crafty look came into the Baron's eyes. "Well now, let me think. You are supposed to be so clever, Tashi. If you really want to help this cur we'll see what you can do. I will set you three simple tasks. If you can carry them out, the dog is yours. What do you say to that?"

'"And if I *can't* do the tasks?" asked Tashi. "What then?"

'"Then *you* will have to kill Pongo yourself."

'Tashi shuddered, but he nodded. What else could he do?

'The Baron paced about the empty cellar. "Let's see now," he chuckled. "Yes, that's it! Task number one: When I return to this room after lunch, I will expect to *hear* you but not see you." He paced some more. He sniggered again as he warmed to his work. "Task number two: I will find Pongo no longer bleeding all over my floor and those ugly cuts will be healed. Task number three – " The Baron's face grew red with rage again. "And THREE: My peacock will be back in my garden ALIVE!"

'The door clanged behind him.

'Tashi sank down on the floor beside Pongo. He gently put the dog's head in his lap and frowned as he stroked the silky ears. It was quite impossible. He sat for an hour staring in front of him, seeing nothing, and then his gaze dropped to his feet. A smile crept over his face.

'"That's task number one," he whispered to Pongo. He leaned back against the wall and looked about the room. His smile grew broader.

'Tashi ran to the far wall where
cobwebs hung thickly in the corner. He
carefully pulled a web down and took it
over to Pongo. It covered his hind
quarters. One by one, Tashi brought the
cobwebs from the wall to the trusting dog
until he was completely covered.

'The bleeding stopped. The thick
cobwebs lay like a bandage on the poor
dog's back. "Now we're getting
somewhere, Pongo!"

'Tashi pulled the little parcel that
Wise-as-an-Owl had given him from his
hair. As he had hoped, it was a teaspoonful
of crushed mandrake root. He popped it
into Pongo's mouth and stood back.
Before his eyes the deep cuts began to
close and heal. In another minute faint
pale scars appeared under the fur – the
only sign of those dreadful wounds. Tashi
gave a shout of joy, but then his smile
faded. He looked into Pongo's trusting
brown eyes and his heart shivered. "How
can I possibly bring the peacock back?"

'Tashi sat down and rested his chin on his knees. The minutes ticked by. He went over the events of yesterday afternoon again and again. He and his friends had come into the garden, the gate had been closed but the peacock was missing. Pongo had bounded over to meet them...

'Later, when the Baron's footsteps sounded outside the cellar, Tashi was ready...

'The Baron stood in the doorway. The room was empty except for Pongo cowering against the far wall. "Big brave Tashi couldn't help you after all, eh mutt? Scampered off home, has he?" sneered the Baron. He peered behind the door. He poked his stick under the bunk bed.

'"No, not at all," a voice answered.

'The Baron spun around and looked behind him. "Wha– where?"

'"See, I'm up here," Tashi called, "having a little walk across the ceiling."

'The Baron's jaw dropped as he looked up and saw Tashi but he quickly recovered and strode over to the dog. He prodded the cobwebs covering Pongo.

'"What's this? Trying to cover up the blood with – Good heavens!" The Baron had another shock as he pulled away the cobwebs to expose the completely healed body of his dog. He swung back to face Tashi. "Well then, smart boy, that just leaves the peacock. Are you going to bring him back to life as well?"

'Tashi bowed. "If you will come with me, Baron, perhaps we will solve the mystery."

'"There's no mystery here," snarled the Baron. "My greedy dog gobbled up a prize peacock and he's going to pay for it."

'But Tashi went out into the garden and began to search around the spot where he had first seen Pongo yesterday. He examined the grass, the fallen leaves and the bushes nearby. He led the Baron down a path past the pavilion to a large thorn bush. And there, caught fast in the branches of the bush, was the peacock. Beside it lay a dead serpent, its body covered in bites.

'"You see, Baron," Tashi said quietly, "Pongo must have seen the snake slither towards your peacock, which ran away, trying to escape. The snake followed for the kill but Pongo must have run up and bravely fought him to the death. He risked his life to protect your property."

'The Baron swallowed and shuffled his feet.

'"But all's well that ends well," Tashi beamed, "because now I have a wonderful loyal dog to take home to my family. Don't I?"

'The Baron nodded glumly. Even he had to admit that a bargain was a bargain.'

Mum threw a pair of socks up in the air and caught them. 'Clever Tashi – he saved that dog's life! I hate it when people are cruel to animals!'

'What dog?' cried Uncle Joe as he walked in the door with Dad. 'Have you got a new dog? Where is it?'

'No, no,' sighed Jack, 'I was just telling a story about one that nearly lost his –'

'Oh I see. That reminds me of the dog
I rescued once from the back of a truck
heading for north Queensland –'

'Were you telling a Tashi story, Jack?'
asked Dad. 'Did I miss out?'

'Yeah, but I've written it down so you can read it.'

'So Tashi brought Pongo home and all Tashi's family were thrilled, I suppose?' asked Mum. 'Particularly Grandfather?'

'That's right. He called Pongo his "Serpent-Slayer" and he saved the best bits of his dinner for him every night. Grandfather said that dog was just about the pluckiest creature on earth, right after his grandson, Tashi.'

'That's true,' agreed Uncle Joe. 'Dogs are brave but then he probably hasn't come across the courage of the well-known African mountain ape. Now when I was in the deep jungle of the Limpopo River I had the opportunity to...'